MY NAME IS COOL!

By Antonio Sacre

Illustrated by Sarah Demonteverde

FAMILIUS

Published by Familius LLC, www.familius.com
PO Box 1249, Reedley, CA 93654.

Familius books are available at special discounts for bulk purchases, whether for sales promotions or for family or corporate use. For more information, email orders@familius.com.

Library of Congress Control Number: 2021952823

Print ISBN 9781641706575
Ebook ISBN 9781641706841
FE 9781641707022
KF 9781641707206

Printed in China
Edited by Michele Robbins
Cover design by Sarah Demonteverde
Book design by Carlos Guerrero

10 9 8 7 6 5 4 3 2 1
First Edition

I've got a bunch of names. A BUNCH! ELEVEN!
How did I get them all?

When I was born, I kept my eyes squeezed shut so tightly that my mom called me "Mr. Magoo" from a cartoon she loved. My papá said I was going to be bilingual, like him, so he called me "El Señor Magoo."

When my tío Tito visited me in the hospital, he said that El Señor Magoo was too long, so he shortened it to "El Goo."

They couldn't put "El Goo" on my birth certificate, so they called me Antonio Bernardo Sacre. Antonio, like my papá, and my abuelo, and my bisabuelo. And Bernardo, after my papá's best friend from Cuba, who could never leave the island, ever. And Sacre, my last name. Three days of life: six names.

3 days old
— 6 names! —

1. Mr. Magoo
2. "El Señor" Magoo
3. El Goo
4. Antonio
5. BERNARDO
6. Sacre

When we arrived home, my abuela grabbed me in her arms and called me "Papito," a name Cuban grandmothers call their nietos.

When my prima Barbara saw me, she hugged and squeezed me. A bunch! She rubbed my head and said, "Coquito," or little coconut head, because my head was small and round and brown, like a coco.

When I learned to walk, I walked fast—really fast—so fast that I bumped into lots and lots of things. I always had little scratches and bruises on my body. One day my tío Miguel noticed my bumps and bruises. He said, "Hola, Futinquito," or old, beat-up, run-down jalopy car that has more dents than you can count. One year old: nine names.

Soon I was all grown up—five years old! The night before my first day of kindergarten, I didn't want to go to school. At all. My papá had an idea. We made a boat of cushions and pillows and went on a sailing adventure. Papá called himself el Comandante, and I chose to be el Capitán.

We sailed all around the world over the sea of words, past the islands of numbers, near the country of shapes. My papá told me I would visit those and even more wonderful places in kindergarten. Now I couldn't wait to go!

As we sailed the waves, a mosquito landed on my papá's rear end. As captain, I had to act. Fast! I smacked it, hard! My papá whooped. I showed him the squashed bug on my hand. He laughed and called me, "El Capitán de los Mosquitos." Five years old: *ten names*!

El Capitán de los Mosquitos

The next morning, I walked to kindergarten all by myself.

Mrs. Green smiled at me and pointed toward an open desk. I sat down. She called off names from a fancy book.

"Mary Smith!"

A girl said, "Here!"

"Darrell Washington!"

"Here!"

Then she called, "Antonio Sacre!"
Everyone looked around the room. I looked too.
"Antonio Sacre?" We all kept searching.

She looked at me, "Honey, are you Antonio Sacre?"

"I don't really think that is my name," I said.

"I'm pretty sure this is you. Aren't you Antonio Sacre?" She squinted at me. "Well . . . ?"

"You must be Antonio, because I found a name for everyone else."

"I think my name is Mr. Magoo El Señor Magoo El Goo Antonio Bernardo Sacre Papito Coquito Futinquito El Capitán de los Mosquitos," I said.

The class giggled.

"Don't be silly, dear, what is your name?"

"My name is Mr. Magoo El Señor Magoo El Goo Antonio Bernardo Sacre Papito Coquito Futinquito El Capitán de los Mosquitos."

The class giggled louder.

"Please, don't cause a fuss on the first day of school. Your name is Antonio Sacre."

Mrs. Green

"Actually, I think my name is more than that. It's—"

But before I could explain, one student in the back of the room said, "Hey, it's Goo-Goo!"
Another said, "Potato!"

Everyone laughed out loud. I kind of laughed too, but I didn't like the nicknames they called me so much.

The teacher looked at me sternly.

"Please walk to the office, talk to the principal, and come back here with a normal name."

I walked into the office. A lady sat in a cozy chair and pointed to a chair across from her.

"I understand there's been a ruckus in Mrs. Green's room."

I nodded.

"What's your name?"

I took a deep breath. I remembered who I was, and I said, "My name is Mr. Magoo El Señor Magoo El Goo Antonio Bernardo Sacre Papito Coquito Futinquito El Capitán de los Mosquitos."

She looked right at me.

"Young man, can you please tell me the story of your names?"

I told her about my whole bunch of names, all ten of them.

She smiled, and her eyes crinkled at the corners. "You, my friend, have a wonderful name, one that you should be proud of. Go back to the classroom and tell Mrs. Green that is your name. And add this one, from me."

She leaned over the desk and whispered in my ear.

I smiled: eleven names!

I raced back to my kindergarten classroom.

"Did you clear up the problem about your name?"
Mrs. Green asked.